# BANG! BANG!

The stagecoach jolted forward.

"Having that box of gold nuggets on board makes me kind of nervous," Grandpa said.

Elizabeth blinked. "Why?"

Grandpa shrugged. "Oh, I don't know. I just wonder about those gunfighters we heard about."

"But Grandpa," Steven said, "that was in the old days. Besides, if there were any gunfighters around, I'd show them."

"You would not!" Jessica said. "You like to brag, but you're just a chicken."

BANG!

Jessica gulped. "That sounded like—"

BANG! BANG!

"Gunshots!" Elizabeth said.

Bantam Skylark Books in the
   SWEET VALLEY KIDS series
Ask your bookseller for the
   books you have missed

SWEET VALLEY KIDS

# THE TWINS AND THE WILD WEST

Written by
Molly Mia Stewart

Created by
FRANCINE PASCAL

Illustrated by
Ying-Hwa Hu

A BANTAM SKYLARK BOOK®
NEW YORK · TORONTO · LONDON · SYDNEY · AUCKLAND

# To Judy Gitenstein

RL 2, 005–008

THE TWINS AND THE WILD WEST
*A Bantam Skylark Book / August 1990*

*Sweet Valley High® and Sweet Valley Kids are trademarks of Francine Pascal*

*Conceived by Francine Pascal*

*Produced by Daniel Weiss Associates, Inc.
33 West 17th Street
New York, NY 10011*

*Cover art by Susan Tang*

*Skylark Books is a registered trademark of Bantam Books, a division of Bantam Doubleday Dell Publishing Group, Inc.*

*Bantam Books are published by Bantam Books, a division of Bantam Double-
day Dell Publishing Group, Inc. Its trademark, consisting of the words
"Bantam Books" and the portrayal of a rooster, is Registered in U.S. Patent
and Trademark Office and in other countries. Marca Registrada. Bantam
Books, 666 Fifth Avenue, New York, New York 10103.*

PRINTED IN THE UNITED STATES OF AMERICA

OPM        0 9 8 7 6 5 4 3 2 1

# CHAPTER 1

# The Surprise Trip

Jessica and Elizabeth Wakefield had their matching suitcases open on their beds. "Are you really taking all those clothes?" Elizabeth asked.

Jessica, who was Elizabeth's identical twin sister, had just chosen a shirt from the closet. She was trying to fit it into her small suitcase on top of the pants, shorts, and T-shirts that were already there. "I wouldn't be taking so many things if I knew where Grandma and Grandpa were taking us," she explained. "I just want to be sure I have the right clothes."

Elizabeth sat down on her bed next to her neatly packed suitcase. "I wish I knew where we were going, too. I'm so curious about our surprise trip."

"And excited," Jessica added. She held up a pink sweatshirt with white cuffs. "Are you packing your sweatsuit?"

Elizabeth nodded. "Yes."

The twins had many matching outfits. Jessica picked hers in pink and Elizabeth usually chose blue. Being identical twins meant that they were alike in many ways. Both girls had long blond hair with bangs and blue-green eyes. Many people had trouble telling them apart. They were the only identical twins in their second-grade class at Sweet Valley Elementary School.

Even though Jessica and Elizabeth looked alike on the outside, they were very different

2

on the inside. Elizabeth liked to read, to write stories, and to play outdoors. She always did her homework on time, and she liked to help her friends.

Jessica was just the opposite. She usually preferred to play indoors with her dolls and stuffed animals. Her favorite part of the school day was recess and talking to her friends. She hated doing homework.

Being different didn't stop Elizabeth and Jessica from being best friends. They loved sharing a bedroom, and they loved sharing pencils and hair ribbons. They even split cookies in half. Being twins was special.

"*I* know where we're going on our trip," said a voice.

The twins looked up in surprise. Their older brother, Steven, was standing in the doorway. He was going with them on their

4

trip. Most of the time he pretended not to know them. The rest of the time he liked to show off.

"OK, Mr. Know-It-All," Jessica said. "If you're so smart, tell us where we're going."

"No way," Steven said. "My lips are sealed," he added, pretending to zip up his lips.

Elizabeth looked at her sister. "Don't listen to him. He doesn't really know."

"Yes I do!" Steven shouted.

Jessica stood in front of him and put her hands on her hips. "Then tell us, smarty," she said. "Are we going to Water Park? Safari Adventure? Camping World?"

Steven looked up at the ceiling. "Did you say something?" he asked after a moment.

Elizabeth rolled her eyes. "Let's finish packing, Jess."

5

The sound of a car door slamming reached their ears.

"It's them!" Jessica shouted. Elizabeth ran to the window and looked out. "Grandma and Grandpa are here!"

Elizabeth, Jessica, and Steven galloped down the stairs. They almost collided with their parents, who were walking to the front door.

"Whoa!" Mr. Wakefield said. "Slow down!"

"Grandma and Grandpa are going to take one look at you three and go right back home," Mrs. Wakefield added, laughing.

Elizabeth stood up straight. "We'll be good," she promised. Jessica and Steven both nodded quickly.

But when the doorbell rang, all three of them shouted happily. "Grandma! Grandpa!"

Mr. Wakefield opened the door. "Hi,

Mother. Hi, Dad," he said, greeting his parents. "Hi!" yelled the twins and Steven. Each one of them hugged their grandparents tightly.

"Well, well," Grandpa Wakefield said with a chuckle. "Who are these wild kids?"

Elizabeth giggled. "*You* know," she said.

"My goodness," Grandma spoke up. "For a moment I thought there was a herd of wild buffaloes in the house. Don't all of you shout at once, now."

"Where are we going?" Jessica jumped up and down with excitement. "We don't even know what to pack."

Grandpa put a finger on his lips for silence. "I guess you didn't notice *this*," he said, pointing to a hat in his other hand. It was a cowboy hat. "Does this give you any ideas?" he asked.

Elizabeth put both hands over her mouth, and her eyes grew wide. "Wild West Town?" she asked.

Instead of answering, Grandpa put the hat on and pointed over his shoulder with his thumb. "Saddle up, cowpokes. It's time to hit the trail."

# CHAPTER 2

# Western Duds for All

"I'm Billy the Kid, and I've got you covered," Steven yelled, aiming his finger at Jessica. His finger was a pretend gun.

Jessica screamed and bounced on the car seat. "Help! Help!" she said, laughing. "Somebody save me!"

"This town ain't big enough for both of us," Elizabeth growled. She pointed her finger at Steven. "Reach for the sky, Billy!"

"Bang! Bang! Bang!" Elizabeth, Jessica, and Steven all made shooting noises. "Pow!" Steven grabbed his stomach and groaned.

Jessica screamed again, and Elizabeth slumped in the seat.

"Not so loud, kids!" Grandma Wakefield scolded from the front seat. "It hurts our ears."

"We're sorry," Elizabeth said, sitting up straight.

The five of them had been driving along the highway toward Wild West Town for two hours. They had another hour to go, and Jessica and Elizabeth and Steven were too excited to sit still.

"Why don't you look at the license plates we pass," Grandma suggested. "Count how many different states you can see."

"There goes one from Arizona!" Steven yelled. "And I saw one from Nevada before."

"No fair!" Jessica said. She kneeled on the

seat to look out the rear window. "All I see are California license plates."

"There goes one from Colorado!" Elizabeth said. "Look!"

"Where?" Jessica said, looking right and left. "I missed it."

"Children!" Their grandmother turned around to look at them. She was smiling, but she looked stern. "If you can't lower your voices, I'm going to ask you for five minutes of silence."

Jessica gulped and looked at her sister. Then she saw her grandfather looking at her through the rear-view mirror. He winked and grinned. That made Jessica giggle.

Before long, the license-plate spotters began to see signs for Wild West Town. Jessica, Elizabeth, and Steven tried to sit still, but it was difficult. By the time Grandpa parked the car, they were squirming to get out.

"We're here," Jessica shouted, clapping her hands.

"Everybody out," Grandpa said. "Our first stop is the Clothing Emporium."

Jessica and Elizabeth hurried to the parking exit and looked around them. The place looked just like a Western movie. Horses were tied up to hitching posts along the street. Women in long dresses were strolling down the street and climbing into wagons. And there were cowboys everywhere.

"What's an emporium?" Elizabeth asked.

"A store," Grandpa explained. "It's right this way," he said, turning the corner.

Jessica skipped along beside her grandfather. "Are we buying clothes?"

"No, just borrowing them," he said. "You'll see."

The group walked into a small store that had racks of clothes and hats along one wall and rows of shoes and boots along the other. A man in a vest and round glasses greeted them. "Good morning," he said with a bow. "My name is Mr. Ferguson. Are you folks new in town?"

"Just passing through for a couple of days," Grandpa answered in a friendly voice. "Me and the missus and these young 'uns are going to need some duds, though."

"What are duds?" Jessica whispered to Elizabeth.

"I think it means clothes," Elizabeth whispered back.

"Look!" Steven shouted. He held up a pair

of chaps from a rack of boys' clothes. The suede pants had fringe up and down the legs. "I'm going to be Billy the Kid for sure."

"Look at this!" Jessica exclaimed. She ran to another rack and pulled out a long, pink dress. "May I wear this?"

"Of course, Jessica," Grandma said. "It will look very pretty on you." She picked a blue dress that matched the pink one. "And how about this for you, Elizabeth?"

Elizabeth bit her lip. "Couldn't . . . couldn't I be a cowgirl?" she asked.

Mr. Ferguson waved his hand. "Take a look at this outfit, little lady."

Elizabeth looked at the pair of red cowgirl boots, red skirt with fringes, and the matching vest Mr. Ferguson held up. He took a red cowgirl hat off a shelf and handed it to Elizabeth.

"I love it," Elizabeth said, putting on the hat.

"It's very tomboyish," Grandma remarked.

"I think she'll look just fine," Grandpa said. He was putting on a tie that looked like a shoelace. Then he put on a vest and coat just like Mr. Ferguson's. "We all will look fine. Now pick your dress, dear, and then we'll see where we can get some lunch in this town."

# CHAPTER 3

# Lunch at the Saloon

Elizabeth tugged her sister's hand. "This way to the Saloon," she said.

"Saloon?" Grandma asked in alarm.

"That's the restaurant," Steven explained. "You said it was time for lunch."

Grandma Wakefield tied her bonnet strings. "Well, I did. But I don't think a saloon is the right place for children."

"Come on, Granny," Grandpa joked. "If we see any gunfights, we'll leave."

"Hooray!" Jessica shouted, twirling around

so that her long skirt swished from side to side. "I'm starving."

Steven tried to rope her with his lasso, but the rope fell on the ground instead. Jessica giggled and ran ahead.

"This is so much fun, Grandma and Grandpa," Elizabeth said. She gave her grandmother a big hug. "Thank you for bringing us here."

Inside the saloon, a few cowboys were playing cards, and a man in a black bowler hat was playing the piano. Several other families who were visiting Wild West Town were already eating lunch. The Wakefields sat down at a large round table and looked at the menus.

"What'll you have, folks?" a waitress in a long dress and apron asked.

Jessica looked quickly at Grandma. "Mom

always lets us order soda when we eat in a restaurant," she said.

Elizabeth's eyes widened. That was a fib. Jessica was trying to get special treatment because they were with their grandparents.

"That's right," Steven said. "I'll have a root beer."

Grandma put down her menu and looked at the waitress. "Milk for the children," she said in a no-nonsense voice.

"But Grandma—" Jessica began.

"Milk," Grandma repeated before Jessica could say anything more.

Grandpa unfolded his napkin and put it on his lap. "May *I* have root beer?" he asked.

"Of course you may," Grandma said, laughing.

Grandpa smiled. "Then I'll have three

glasses of root beer, please," he said to the waitress. "And bring them all at the same time. I'm extra thirsty today."

Grandma shook her head while Elizabeth and Jessica looked at each other. They knew Grandpa was going to give the root beer to them.

"Grandpa, may I go talk to the cowboys?" Steven asked.

"Yes, Steven," Grandpa said.

Elizabeth sat up straight. "May I go, too?"

"No way," Steven answered quickly. "Girls in the old days didn't do anything but cook and sew," he said bossily. "So cowboys wouldn't want to talk to you."

"But I'm a cowgirl," Elizabeth pointed out.

"Now, now, kids," Grandma said. "Steven

you go. Elizabeth won't mind staying with us, will you dear?"

Elizabeth tried not to look disappointed as she watched Steven walk over to the cowboys with a triumphant smile on his face. She didn't want her grandparents to think she was having a bad time.

"Can we ride the ponies?" Jessica asked.

"Only if it's on a nice, quiet pony," Grandma said.

Jessica picked up her fork and pretended to trot it around her place mat. "I want to ride a black pony with a white star on its nose," she said.

Grandpa winked at the twins. "If you girls want pony rides, you'll have pony rides."

"Thank you," Jessica and Elizabeth said at the same time.

"Maybe we'll even get your grandmother in the saddle," Grandpa added. He took Grandma's hand and gave it an affectionate squeeze.

A rope dropped suddenly around Jessica's shoulders. "Hey!" she yelled.

"Yahoo!" Steven let out a whoop and ran over. "I did it. I roped Jessica."

He raised his fists in the air and danced around in a circle. "Girls are so dumb," Steven said. "It sure must have been boring to be a girl in the Wild West."

"No way!" Elizabeth said, jumping out of her chair.

"Yes way!" Steven insisted.

Jessica stood up, too. "You're the big dummy, Steven."

Grandma spoke up. "No one is dumb. Now

please sit down, all of you," she said. "Our lunch is here."

Elizabeth frowned. She was angry at Steven. She would show him that girls weren't dumb. She would make Steven take back what he had said.

# CHAPTER 4

# Wild West Town

After lunch all five of the Wakefields began their tour of Wild West Town. First they saw a blacksmith putting new shoes on a horse. Then they watched a woman printing a newspaper on an old-fashioned printing press. They helped two men fix a wagon wheel. They also visited the town post office, the general store, and the barber shop.

In the stagecoach office, there was a telegraph machine. Grandpa explained that it was used to send messages before the telephone was invented. Elizabeth tried it out. The machine made a lot of clicking sounds.

"Did you use these when you were growing up?" Jessica asked Grandma.

"Goodness, no!" Grandma laughed. "This is what it was like a hundred years ago. I wasn't alive then!"

"Did they still have stagecoaches when you were little?" Steven wanted to know.

"We had cars," Grandpa told them. "Of course, they weren't as fast and fancy as the ones we drive now."

Elizabeth looked out the window as a woman rode by on a horse. "I wish we still used horses instead of cars," she said. "It would be much more fun."

"May I get a souvenir horse?" Jessica asked. "I saw them for sale in the saloon.

Please? Mom lets us buy souvenirs when we go on trips."

Grandma began shaking her head. "Don't go buying the first thing you see," she said. "You may find something even nicer."

"Your grandmother's right," Grandpa said. "I'll give you each three dollars so you can buy your own souvenirs. But choose carefully."

"Hooray!" they all cheered.

"And don't spend too much on candy or you'll feel sick," Grandma said quickly. "Get some nice postcards."

Elizabeth frowned. "Do I have to?"

"Get what you want," Grandpa said, tugging her ponytail. "But first, there's something across the street I think we should do."

"What?" Steven asked.

Grandpa headed for the door. "Come on, cowpokes."

Elizabeth and Jessica giggled and followed their grandfather. Across the street was a sign that read MASON'S PHOTOGRAPHY PARLOR. Inside, a man with a long mustache greeted them and had them sit on an old-fashioned sofa. Then he stood behind a large square camera and covered his head with a dark cloth. "Say 'Wild West,'" he said.

"Wild West," they all said together. A flashbulb popped and made them blink.

Jessica, Elizabeth, and Steven crowded around Mr. Mason. The instant photograph began to develop, but instead of being in color, it was brown and gray and white.

"How come it looks like that?" Steven asked.

"That's how photos used to look," Grandma said. "Let's take one more. That way Grandpa and I can keep one, and we can give the other to your parents."

After sitting for another photograph, they continued their tour of Wild West Town. By dinner time, the twins and Steven were so tired they could hardly keep their eyes open at the table.

"We don't have to go to bed until nine o'clock," Jessica said sleepily.

"Oh, really?" Grandma asked, raising her eyebrows.

Elizabeth nudged Jessica with her elbow. Their bedtime was eight-thirty.

"Really," Jessica said.

Grandma put down her menu. "Well, your mother told me eight-thirty," she said. "And anyway, you look very sleepy to me. I'd be surprised if you were even able to stay up until eight."

Jessica put on a pouty expression, but Elizabeth didn't mind. "It doesn't matter," she said. "I think I'm going to fall asleep before dinner even comes."

"Baby," Steven teased.

Grandpa laughed. "Well, we *all* need a good night's sleep," he said. "We've got a big day ahead of us tomorrow."

"What are we going to do?" Jessica asked.

"It's a surprise," Grandma said. "A Wild West surprise."

Elizabeth giggled and then yawned a wide yawn. She was having so much fun, she didn't mind not knowing. She knew that the faster she ate and went to bed, the sooner it would be tomorrow.

# CHAPTER 5

# The Big Day

"OK. It's tomorrow. Tell us the surprise!" Jessica said the next morning at breakfast.

Grandma took a sip of her coffee. "Should we tell?" she asked Grandpa.

"Yes. Tell us," Elizabeth said.

Steven was twirling his lasso by his chair. "Yes! Can't we know?"

"Please? Pretty please?" Jessica begged.

"Oh, all right," Grandpa said. His eyes twinkled. "We're going on a stagecoach . . ."

"Wow!" Steven gasped.

". . . to visit a gold mine," Grandpa finished.

Elizabeth stared at him. "For real?" she asked.

Grandma nodded. "For real. Now eat up. The stage leaves in fifteen minutes."

"We'd better hurry." Jessica quickly scooped the last of her cereal into her mouth, while Elizabeth gulped down her orange juice.

Fifteen minutes later, the group stood outside the stage office. "Is it a real gold mine?" Jessica asked.

"Yes, but it's all played out," their grandfather said. "That means there's only a little bit of gold left in it."

Elizabeth pushed her cowgirl hat down tightly on her head so it wouldn't fall off. She wanted to be ready for anything.

32

Pretty soon, there was a thunder of hoof-beats, and the stagecoach came rolling around the corner in a cloud of dust. "Whoa!" the driver yelled as he pulled on the reins. "This is the stage to Dead Man's Mine! All aboard!"

"May I ride up on top with the driver?" Steven asked.

"Oh, me too," Elizabeth said.

Grandpa shrugged. "If it's OK with the driver, it's OK with me."

"I'm riding inside where it isn't so dusty," Jessica announced. "OK, Grandma?"

"It's fine with me, dear," Grandma replied with a smile.

Elizabeth and Steven climbed up on the seat with the driver. "Howdy, *pardners*," the driver said with a nod. "My name's Jesse."

"Wow. Like Jesse James?" Steven asked.

33

"This is my little sister. She's trying to dress like a real cowboy."

Elizabeth frowned. "Quit making fun of me," she said, sitting down beside her brother. "My twin sister's name is Jessica, and sometimes we call her Jessie," she said to the driver.

Jesse flicked his long whip, and the stagecoach set off with a jerk. "This is fun!" Elizabeth yelled.

The stage raced down the main street of Wild West Town and then headed out into the open country. After passing a few homesteads and going uphill for a while, the stage stopped outside the old mine.

Jessica grabbed Elizabeth's hand as they walked into the mine's dark tunnel. Jesse carried an old-fashioned lantern that cast spooky shadows on the walls of the mine. "In its heyday, this mine put out thousands of dollars worth of gold ore each month," he said. "Hundreds of men worked here to get the metal out of the mountain. Of course, there were some folks who wanted the gold without doing the hard work themselves." He paused before adding, "If you know what I mean."

Steven's eyes widened. "You mean bandits?" he asked.

Jesse nodded solemnly and then started walking again.

"Do you think there're any bad guys still around?" Jessica whispered to Elizabeth.

Elizabeth shook her head. "I don't think so." But she held her twin sister's hand even tighter. It was scary and dark in the tunnel, and she didn't want to get lost, especially if there were bandits around.

When they came out of the mine, Jesse took them down to a sparkling stream. "I'll show you how to pan for gold," he said. He took a shallow pan and dipped it into the gravel. Then he swished the water back and forth, before holding out the pan.

"Look," Jessica said. At the bottom were tiny, gold flecks that glittered. "Is it real gold?"

"Sure is," Jesse answered. "Now you give it a try."

Grandma and Grandpa Wakefield watched as the twins and Steven panned for gold. Jessica kept getting the hem of her dress wet in the stream, and Steven teased her. "I told you, girls never would have done this in the old days," he said. "You should have stayed home."

"Just you wait, Steven," Elizabeth said.

"You'll see. I could have been a cowboy, too. Or even a sheriff."

Steven snickered. "Sure, little Lizzie."

Elizabeth and Jessica looked at each other. They would show him girls could do anything boys could do.

# CHAPTER 6

# Stick 'em Up

Elizabeth, Jessica, and Steven panned for gold for almost an hour while Grandma and Grandpa Wakefield sat in the sun. They were all having a wonderful time. Jessica scooped some gravel into her pan and swirled the water around. She could see a few sparkles of gold dust in the bottom, but that was all.

"I'm going over there," she said, pointing to a large rock on the river bank.

"Jessica!" Grandma called. "Stay where I can see you."

"But, Grandma—" Jessica began.

"I don't want you to slip and hurt yourself," Grandma warned.

Jessica frowned and walked back to join Elizabeth, who was still looking for gold. "Grandma hardly lets us do anything at all," she grumbled, as she sat down next to her sister. "It's not fair."

Elizabeth shrugged. "But Mom wouldn't let you climb on those rocks, either."

"I know that," Jessica said. "But I thought Grandma would let us do special stuff since we're not at home."

"I know." Elizabeth looked into her pan. "Look! There's a tiny bit of gold in here," she said.

"Stick 'em up," growled Steven, as he came up behind them. His bandanna covered his face below his eyes and he was aiming a make-believe gun at them. "Give me all your gold."

"Go away," Jessica said.

"Finish up, kids," Grandpa called. "The stage is going to leave in a few minutes."

Jessica emptied her pan and climbed up the bank. Her long dress kept tripping her, so Elizabeth helped her along.

"Slowpokes," Steven teased.

"Let's ignore him," Jessica said.

"Everybody rides inside on this trip," Grandma announced as they walked toward the stagecoach.

Steven's mouth dropped open. "But—"

"No buts," Grandma said. "Everybody inside."

"See what I mean?" Jessica whispered to Elizabeth. Elizabeth looked disappointed, but she didn't say anything.

41

"Be careful, folks," said Jesse. He lifted a heavy box onto the roof of the stagecoach. "We're carrying a shipment of gold nuggets," he explained.

"Wow," Jessica said.

"Why can't I ride on top, Grandma?" Steven asked. "I'm Billy the Kid, and I can help guard the gold."

Grandpa patted Steven's shoulder. "You heard your grandmother, partner."

"Yes, I heard," Steven grumbled. He climbed inside the coach.

When they were all settled inside, Jesse cracked the whip. "Giddyap!" he yelled to the horses. The coach jolted forward.

"Isn't this a nice ride?" Grandma asked everyone.

Elizabeth, Jessica, and Steven nodded but

didn't say anything. They were all sulking.

"It's very pleasant, indeed," Grandpa said with a smile. "Of course, having that box of gold nuggets on board makes me kind of nervous."

Elizabeth blinked. "Why?"

Grandpa shrugged. "Oh, I don't know. I just wonder about those gunfighters Jesse was telling us about. That's all."

"But Grandpa," Steven said, "that was in the old days."

Grandpa laughed. "You're right."

"Besides," Steven added, "if there were any gunfighters still around, I'd show them."

"Sure, sure, Steven," Elizabeth said, rolling her eyes.

"I would too," Steven yelled back.

"You would not!" Jessica said. "You like to brag, but you're just a chicken."

Steven frowned. "You take that back, Jessica!"

"Kids!" Grandma said. "Stop shouting right this—"

BANG! A loud noise interrupted her. Everyone looked around in surprise.

Jessica gulped. "That sounded like—"

BANG! BANG!

"Gunshots!" Elizabeth said.

The horses started galloping, and everyone inside the coach began to bounce up and down. They could hear more shots and more yelling outside, but there was so much dust they couldn't see anything through the windows.

Suddenly the coach stopped.

"Grandma," Jessica whispered, grabbing her grandmother's hand.

"Just sit still," Grandma said in a low voice. "Don't say a word."

"Everybody out of the coach!" yelled a loud, angry-sounding voice. "And keep your hands up where I can see them. This is a holdup!"

# CHAPTER 7

# Black Bill

Elizabeth's stomach flip-flopped. She stared at her sister, who looked very frightened. "Just do what he tells you," Grandpa said quickly. "Don't do anything to make him angry."

Grandpa opened the door of the stagecoach and put his hands up in the air. "OK, OK, we're coming out." He jumped down, and Grandma followed him.

"There's no one inside except three children," she said. "Please leave them alone."

"Children?" the outlaw roared. "Tell them

to get out here this minute. No one gets special treatment when Black Bill holds up the stage."

Jessica let out a squeak and grabbed Elizabeth's hand.

"Come on," Elizabeth whispered. Steven took a deep breath. "We're coming," he said. His voice shook a little bit.

Elizabeth and Jessica jumped down to the ground. Facing them was a tall man dressed in black. He wore a black hat, a black bandanna across his face, a black shirt, black pants, and black boots. A black horse was standing behind him, breathing hard and stamping one foot.

"Give me all your money and all your jewelry," Black Bill growled. "And no dilly dallying, now!"

Jessica looked angry. "But I only have two

47

dollars and fifty cents. I need it to buy souvenirs."

Black Bill laughed. "Don't give me any hard luck stories, kid. And don't try any funny business, you," he said, spinning around to look at Grandpa. "Reach for the sky."

"I'm not doing anything," Grandpa said, putting his hands up higher.

"You'd better not," Black Bill said. "Any tricks and you'll all be walking back to town barefoot."

Jesse, the stagecoach driver, was still sitting up on the coach seat, with his hands in the air. He looked scared. "Listen B-B-B-Black Bill," he stammered. "D-d-d-don't harm these nice folks. Just take the gold and leave us in peace."

"Oh, I'll take the gold all right," Black Bill

shouted. "And everything else, too. Now hurry it up!"

He took two steps closer to Grandma. "Let me have your jewelry, Granny."

Elizabeth stepped in front of her grandmother and faced Black Bill. "Don't talk to my grandma that way," she said loudly. She was scared, but she was angry, too.

"That's right," Jessica piped up. She pointed her finger at Black Bill. "You're a very mean man, so go away and leave my family alone."

Black Bill let out a whoop. "Go away and leave you alone?" he repeated. He slapped his thigh. "I'd like to see you make me, little lady." He let out another big laugh.

Jessica looked at Elizabeth and Elizabeth looked at Jessica. As quick as a wink, Jessica

stomped hard on Black Bill's toes. He let out a loud yell. "Oooow!" he howled, hopping around on one foot.

Quickly, Elizabeth grabbed the brim of Black Bill's hat and yanked it down over his eyes. Then Jessica kicked him hard in the shins.

"Jessica!" Grandpa gasped.

"Elizabeth!" Grandma screamed.

"Steven!" Elizabeth shouted. "Get the lasso!"

Steven was so startled that he stood frozen for a moment. Then he ran forward and started wrapping his lasso around Black Bill. In three seconds flat, the bandit was tied up like a package.

"Let me go, you crazy kids," Black Bill yelled.

51

Elizabeth looked at her brother and dusted off her hands. "I told you that girls could do anything, Steven." She put her hands on her hips and smiled proudly.

# CHAPTER 8

# The New Deputy Sheriffs

Jesse was staring at them all with his mouth wide open. He shook his head in disbelief. "What are you kids doing?" Black Bill shouted. He was trying to get the rope loose, but it didn't budge. "Let me go! Untie me!"

"No way," Steven said, acting tough and brave now that the danger had passed. "We've got you right where we want you."

"Well I'll be a monkey's uncle," Grandpa said quietly. He, too, shook his head, and let out a whistle.

"Didn't we do a good job?" Jessica asked, beaming.

Grandma and Grandpa looked at each other and smiled.

"It was a very brave thing to do, kids," Grandpa said. "You tackled that bandit all by yourselves."

Elizabeth and Jessica and Steven smiled from ear to ear.

"But you must promise us one thing," Grandma said seriously. "Don't ever, ever, *ever* do that with a real robber."

Elizabeth, Jessica, and Steven just looked at each other in surprise. They didn't understand what Grandma was saying.

"A real robber?" Elizabeth finally said.

"Wasn't Black Bill a real robber?" Jessica whispered.

Grandpa chuckled. "It's all part of Wild West Town. It's all make-believe, remember?"

Elizabeth and Jessica stared at each other. They had been so excited about the stagecoach ride and the trip to the mine that they had thought Black Bill was a real outlaw.

"The holdup was just part of the ride," Grandma explained with a warm smile. "We wanted it to be a big surprise for you."

"It sure was," Steven said. His cheeks were pink, but he laughed.

"And Black Bill is the one who got the biggest surprise of all," Grandpa said. Everyone laughed.

"But that doesn't change one thing," Grandma said. "You really thought you were protecting Grandpa and me, and that makes us very proud of you. If I didn't already love you all as much as I do, I'd love you even more."

Elizabeth felt a little bit embarrassed, but she felt happy, too. First, Steven wouldn't be able to make fun of girls anymore. Also, they had made Grandma and Grandpa very proud.

"OK, Black Bill," Jesse spoke up. He climbed down and took the end of the rope. "Get up on top of the stage. I'm taking you to the sheriff."

"I'll get you," Black Bill growled. But his growl wasn't very tough anymore. He climbed up and sat quietly in the seat next to Jesse.

"All right, folks," Jesse said. "Let's head back to town. I have a feeling the sheriff will want to give you three heroes a nice reward."

When they arrived back in town, Jesse turned over Black Bill to Sheriff Graham. "I've been trying to catch this varmint for a long time," the sheriff told the Wakefields. "I guess I should make you three young 'uns honorary deputies."

"But we know it was just make-believe," Jessica said.

The sheriff winked. "But you still caught Black Bill fair and square. *That's* not make-believe. Come on into the jailhouse for a minute."

Elizabeth and Jessica followed the sheriff into his office. Steven and their grandparents were right behind them.

"I've got some extra badges here," the sheriff said, reaching into his desk drawer. "Here they are."

Sheriff Graham took out three silver stars and pinned one each on Elizabeth, Jessica, and Steven. "Raise your right hands," he said. "Do you solemnly swear to uphold the law and

carry out the duties of a deputy sheriff of Wild West Town?"

"Yes," Jessica, Elizabeth, and Steven said together.

"Then congratulations," Sheriff Graham said. "Now let's head over to the saloon. I'm buying ice cream cones for each of you."

# CHAPTER 9

# Rodeo Fun

"This is the most fun I've ever had," Jessica said at dinner. "Me, too," Elizabeth agreed.

Grandma and Grandpa smiled. "We're so glad you're having a good time," Grandma said.

Steven polished his deputy badge with his napkin. "Wait till I tell the guys at school about how I captured Black Bill."

"How *you* captured him?" Grandpa asked. "You've got a good imagination, my boy."

"I mean, how *we* did," Steven said. Steven

looked around the table. Elizabeth and Jessica glared at their brother. Steven's face turned red. "I mean, how Elizabeth and Jessica did," he added quickly.

"That's better," Jessica said with a big smile.

"But I helped tie him up," Steven said.

"You're all heroes," Grandma said. "Each one of you was very brave." She lifted her glass of root beer. "I propose a toast."

Each of them raised their glasses, too.

"Here's to our wonderful weekend at Wild West Town," Grandma said.

They all clinked their glasses together.

"I want to come back again," Elizabeth said. Jessica nodded.

"I'm sure your mom and dad will bring you," Grandpa said.

Elizabeth looked at Jessica, and they both

looked at Steven. Elizabeth shook her head. "No. We want to come back with you," she said, smiling at her grandparents.

Grandpa laughed. "Well, that deserves another toast." They all clinked glasses again.

"Oh my goodness," Grandma said, looking at her watch. "If we want to go to the rodeo, we have to hurry up."

"Rodeo?" Steven gasped.

*"Rodeo?"* Elizabeth said.

"RODEO!" Jessica shouted.

Grandma smiled. "Rodeo," she repeated. "It's the perfect way to end a perfect weekend. And afterward, there'll be pony rides," she said, smiling at Jessica.

As soon as they were finished with dinner, they hurried out of the saloon. Almost everyone in town was heading toward the rodeo ring. Elizabeth noticed that many of the other kids her age were looking at her silver badge. "I'll bet they're wondering how we became deputies," she said to Jessica.

Jessica beamed. "You have to catch Black Bill, first. And that's not easy."

The rodeo ring had bleachers up all around. In the ring, three cowgirls were doing tricks on pinto ponies. They did handstands on the saddles, and stood on one leg while the ponies cantered around the ring.

"I want to be a cowgirl when I grow up," Jessica said.

Suddenly the gates opened and about twenty cowboys galloped into the ring on their horses. Some waved their hats and twirled their lassos and others yelled and fired their pistols. The crowd stood and cheered.

A cowboy wearing a white shirt and red vest rode by and tipped his hat at the crowd.

"It's Black Bill!" Jessica shouted, jumping from her seat. Black Bill looked much friendlier without his black clothes on. He smiled and waved at the Wakefields and then rode away.

"He's not really a bad guy," Elizabeth reminded Jessica. "But he is a real cowboy."

The rodeo was exciting. The cowboys rode bucking broncos, and then they roped calves. One cowboy even rode a large bucking bull.

When the show was over, Jessica, Elizabeth, Steven, and the other kids visiting Wild West Town rode ponies around the ring.

"Make sure you don't fall off, Steven," Elizabeth shouted. Steven was riding ahead of her. She and Jessica laughed as he bounced in his saddle.

"If you fall off," Jessica said, "we'll take your deputy badge away."

Steven didn't answer. He was having too much trouble staying on his pony.

Jessica and Elizabeth looked at each other and laughed. They weren't going to let their brother *ever* get away with teasing them again.

# CHAPTER 10

# Home Sweet Home

"We're home!" Elizabeth yelled, opening the front door. "Mommy! Dad!" Jessica set her suitcase down with a thump, while Steven ran up the stairs. Grandma and Grandpa shut the front door behind them.

"Well, well, well! Welcome home," Mrs. Wakefield said, coming down the stairs. She gave Jessica and Elizabeth each a hug and a kiss. "We missed you. Did you have a good time?"

"It was great," Jessica said cheerfully. "We didn't want to leave."

Mr. Wakefield walked into the front hall and kissed the twins. "I'm glad you had fun, girls. The house was very quiet without you. Where's Steven?"

"Here I am!" Steven shouted, running down the stairs.

"Dad, look," Elizabeth said, pointing to her deputy badge. "We all got one for capturing Black Bill."

Mr. Wakefield raised his eyebrows and looked at Grandma and Grandpa. "Who's Black Bill?" he asked.

"Let's just say Black Bill is one sorry bandit," Grandpa said. "The kids really got into the spirit of the wild West."

"And they were very brave," Grandma added.

Jessica hugged her father's leg and looked up at him. "We wore costumes, and rode in a stagecoach, and panned for gold, and ate in a saloon, and got our picture taken like in the old days, and we want to go back," she said, running out of breath.

"Can we?" Elizabeth asked, hugging Mr. Wakefield's other leg. "Next weekend?"

"Please?" Jessica chimed in. "Can Grandma and Grandpa take us again next weekend?"

"Whoa! Hold your horses." Mr. Wakefield laughed. "You should ask them, not me."

Jessica let go of her father, and tugged at Grandpa's hand. "I'm not letting go until you say yes."

"Well, maybe not next weekend," Grandpa said with a chuckle. "But now that the out-laws are all gone, I guess it's safe for us to go back soon."

"For now," Grandma said, "Why don't you take your saddlebags and go unpack your duds?"

Elizabeth smiled and picked up her suitcase. "Come on, partner," she said to Jessica. "Let's hit the trail."

Elizabeth and Jessica wore their deputy sheriff's badges to school on Monday.

As soon as they walked into their classroom, Jessica shouted. "Look, everyone! We're deputies of Wild West Town."

A crowd of kids gathered around to see. "How come I didn't get a badge when I went?" Todd Wilkins asked.

"You didn't capture Black Bill," Jessica said proudly.

"Who's Black Bill?" Eva and Amy asked at once.

Elizabeth took a deep breath. "He's an outlaw, except he isn't really one in real life—"

"And he held up the stagecoach," Jessica went on. "And we captured him ourselves."

"Weren't you scared?" Ellen Riteman asked. She shivered. "It sounds dangerous."

"I wouldn't be scared," Winston Egbert said firmly.

"Did you ride a horse?" Lila wanted to know.

"Yes," Elizabeth answered with a smile.

She looked around at the others. Almost the whole class was listening to them.

Lois Waller was standing at the edge of the group. Her eyes were wide with interest. She spoke up. "You're so brave to go on a horse."

"It wasn't a very big horse," Elizabeth explained. "It was just a pony."

"Lois wouldn't even go on a rocking

71

horse," Lila teased. "She's too much of a chicken!"

"They don't have horses with training wheels," Charlie added. Everyone laughed. They all knew Lois still had training wheels on her bicycle.

Lois' eyes filled with tears. She cried at almost everything, especially when someone teased her. Sniffling, she walked away and sat at her desk.

Elizabeth felt sorry for Lois. Lois was friendly and nice, but she was afraid of everything. Could Elizabeth do anything to help Lois become braver?

*Will Lois ever be able to stop kids from teasing her? Find out in Sweet Valley Kids #11, CRYBABY LOIS.*

## SWEET VALLEY KIDS™

# COULD *YOU* BE THE NEXT SWEET VALLEY READER OF THE MONTH?

## ENTER BANTAM BOOKS' SWEET VALLEY CONTEST & SWEEPSTAKES IN ONE!

### Calling all Sweet Valley Fans! Here's a chance to appear in a Sweet Valley book!

We know how important Sweet Valley is to you. That's why we've come up with a Sweet Valley celebration offering exciting opportunities to have YOUR thoughts printed in a Sweet Valley book!

### "How do I become a Sweet Valley Reader of the Month?"

It's easy. Just write a one-page essay (no more than 150 words, please) telling us a little about yourself, and why you like to read Sweet Valley books. We will pick the best essays and print them along with the winner's photo in the back of upcoming Sweet Valley books. Every month there will be a new Sweet Valley Kids Reader of the Month!

### And, there's more!

Just sending in your essay makes you eligible for the Grand Prize drawing for a trip to Los Angeles, California! This once-in-a-life-time trip includes round-trip airfare, accommodations for 5 nights (economy double occupancy), a rental car, and meal allowance. (Approximate retail value: $4,500.)

Don't wait! Write your essay today.
No purchase necessary. See the next page for Official rules.

AN 144 SVK

# ENTER BANTAM BOOKS' SWEET VALLEY READER OF THE MONTH SWEEPSTAKES

# SWEET VALLEY KIDS

Jessica and Elizabeth have had lots of adventures in *Sweet Valley High* and *Sweet Valley Twins*...now read about the twins at age seven! You'll love all the fun that comes with being seven—birthday parties, playing dress-up, class projects, putting on puppet shows and plays, losing a tooth, setting up lemonade stands, caring for animals and much more! It's all part of SWEET VALLEY KIDS. Read them all!

☐ **SURPRISE! SURPRISE! #1**
15758-2     $2.75/$3.25

☐ **RUNAWAY HAMSTER #2**
15759-0     $2.75/$3.25

☐ **THE TWINS' MYSTERY TEACHER # 3**
15760-4     $2.75/$3.25

☐ **ELIZABETH'S VALENTINE # 4**
15761-2     $2.75/$3.25

☐ **JESSICA'S CAT TRICK # 5**
15768-X     $2.75/$3.25

☐ **LILA'S SECRET # 6**
15773-6     $2.75/$3.25

☐ **JESSICA'S BIG MISTAKE # 7**
15799-X     $2.75/$3.25

☐ **JESSICA'S ZOO ADVENTURE # 8**
15802-3     $2.75/$3.25

☐ **ELIZABETH'S SUPER-SELLING LEMONADE #9**
15807-4     $2.75/$3.25